An **Andrex** Publication

PUPPY GOES
TO
THE ZOO

Written by
Gerald Durrell

Illustrated by Cliff Wright

Hello, I'm Puppy, and Nick and Susan are my family, with Mum, Dad and Grandad. We do lots of exciting things together.

One day, I was rolling around the garden and Nick and Susan were tickling my tummy, which is great fun. Then Susan said, "Grandad's going to take us to the zoo. And you're coming too, Puppy."

I wondered what a zoo was.

"A zoo is where lots of different animals from all over the world live," said Susan. "It's a safe place for some animals because, in the countries they come from, their wild homes are being destroyed to make room for more people. So these poor animals have nowhere to live any more."

"Puppies aren't usually allowed in zoos," Nick explained, "but as a special treat Mr Green, who owns the zoo, will let you come in with us."

"He'll let you in because you've had all those special jabs from the vet," Susan said.

Wow, I thought, a trip to the zoo to meet all the different animals! I was so excited, I dashed about the hall singing and then I ran through Grandad's feet and nearly knocked him over.

Grandad just chuckled because he's used to me.

When we got to the zoo,
I didn't know where to look
first.

There were so many animals.
All the birds were different
colours. There was one with
a very long tail and feathers
of blue and gold and a great
curved beak.

"I'm Parrot," he squawked,
looking down at me.

"I'm Puppy," I said. "Where do you come from?"

"I come from the great forests of Brazil," he said.

"Is that near here?" I asked.

"No," said Parrot. "It's thousands of miles away. I'm the most beautiful bird there, maybe the most beautiful bird in the world."

"Oh no you're not!" said a bird all pink and red with a harsh quack, who said her name was Flamingo. "I'm the most beautiful bird in the world."

"No you're not," shrilled a bird called Peacock. "Look at my tail. Everyone in India where I come from says I'm the most beautiful."

They all started screeching and showing off.

"Stop it, all of you,"
Heron honked. He was a
tall grey bird with a long beak.
"Puppy, you decide."

What could I do? "Well, you're all
lovely," I said, "so I can't choose."

"That's true," said Heron, and they
all agreed. I said goodbye quickly.

Then I got a huge fright! There in front of me, standing in a pond, was the biggest animal I had ever seen. It seemed as big as a bus and it had grey wrinkly skin and enormous ears.

Its nose was like a long wrinkled hosepipe.

"Wow! What's your name?" I asked.

"I'm Elephant," he said in a rumbly sort of voice like thunder. "I'm the wisest of all the animals, and I'm the biggest animal on the land. The only animal bigger than me is Blue Whale who lives in the sea."

"Where do you come from?" I asked.

"From Africa," he replied, "and I have cousins who live in India."

"You're so big, you must eat lots."

"Oh yes," said Elephant, "I have to eat tons of food to keep my strength up. I eat lots of hay, turnips, fruit, bread, carrots and things like that."

"I couldn't eat all that," I said.

Another big strange animal had the longest neck I had ever seen.

"Hello," she said in a soft voice, looking down at me with big brown eyes. "You're Puppy, aren't you? I am so tall I saw you coming and I asked who you were."

"Why do you have such a long neck?" I asked.

"Ah," she said, "we Giraffes like to eat only tiny fresh leaves from the tops of trees. We have had to grow our necks very long so that we can get to the tree tops without needing to climb up them."

"That's clever," I said.

I scampered along the path and saw a fierce
looking animal with a lot of dark fur round
his head and shoulders. He roared at me.

"I'm Lion, King of the Jungle, and I eat puppies
like you for breakfast."

Next door was a giant cat with black stripes.

When he heard what Lion said, he got into a rage.
"You're not King of the Jungle. That's me, Tiger,
and I could eat a puppy for breakfast and dinner."

"I am King of the Jungle," roared Lion, "and I
could eat a puppy for breakfast, dinner and tea."

Eat me for breakfast! No thanks...

I ran away quickly and, on an island in a pond close by, I met a lot of much friendlier animals swinging through the branches of the trees. "Ooh, Ooh, Ooh," they chattered.

"We're the Monkeys," they said. "Take no notice of Lion and Tiger."

"But they said they could eat me for breakfast, dinner and tea," I said.

"Rubbish," said one of the Monkeys. "Some of their family are fierce, but those two wouldn't hurt a fly."

"Phew!" I said. "I'd hate to end up inside a lion or a tiger."

"No danger of that. Ooh, Ooh, Ooh!" The Monkeys went swinging off through the trees.

On the way I talked to lots of other animals too. There were big furry growly bears, crocodiles with long sharp teeth and many different kinds of monkeys.

With the help of my nose, I tracked down Susan, Nick and Grandad.

"Puppy, where have you been?" asked Nick.

They were talking to Mr Green who owns the zoo.
"Someone left the gate open," he said, "and we
can't find the tortoise anywhere."

There was Peep! Peep! from the tiny train that
carried people around the zoo and stopped at
different places. I went to see and I nearly
got in its way.

I scrambled to the side of the
track, and flopped
down onto a large
stone. Only it wasn't a
stone........it moved.
Then it grunted.

"Who are you?" I panted.

"I'm Tortoise," he said in a hoarse sort of voice. "I'm just going to cross the railway line on my way home."

"Puppy!" shouted Nick. I jumped. They had all come to find me.

"Look at that," said Grandad.

"He's found the tortoise!" cried Nick and Susan.

"And he stopped him from crossing the railway line where a train might have squashed him as flat as a pancake," said Mr Green.

"You're a hero," said Nick and Susan.

Wow, I'm a hero, I thought.

We all went back to the zoo, and Grandad bought ice creams all round. It was so cold it almost froze my nose. But it was delicious.

When we got home I rushed into the garden and told my friend Blackbird all about the zoo and how I saved Tortoise.

"It sounds wonderful," he said, "but with all those colourful birds I'm afraid I would look very dull."

"You're a lovely glossy black," I said, "and you have a bright yellow beak. You're as beautiful as any of them."

"Are you sure, Puppy?" asked Blackbird, cheering up. "Maybe I'll fly down to the zoo one day and meet some of your new friends."

"Yes, you should," I said, with a huge yawn. "It's great."

As I lay in my basket, each member of the family came and patted me as usual and told me how clever I had been to find and save Tortoise. So I went to sleep, a tired but happy hero.